My Friend Isabelle

Eliza Woloson

Illustrated by Bryan Gough

Woodbine House 2003

My
name
is
Charlie.

This is my
friend Isabelle.

Even though we are the same age,

I am tall.

Isabelle is short.

I run fa *s* *t* .

Isabelle
takes
her
time.

I carry around a black and
white kitty and Isabelle carries
around a doll
named Meg.

I know a lot of words.

Isabelle's words

are sometimes hard

for me

to understand.

Mommy says that differences are what make the world so great.

Every Friday Isabelle and I play together.

We dance to Stevie Wonder. Isabelle teaches me

how to ...

t w i r l.

We pretend to go shopping
for grapes at the store.
We cry when one of us
forgets to share.

We drink apple juice and eat Cheerios at the little red table and chairs.

We bring our sippy cups together and say "CHEERS!"

Kitty and Meg say "CHEERS!" too.

We

go

down

the

big

slide

at

the

park...

We both
like to
do it
ourselves.

We hold hands.

Isabelle
has
soft hands.

Mommy is right.

Isabelle is a child with Down syndrome. This means she doesn't look or think quite like Charlie does. Isabelle can do many things that Charlie can do but sometimes it takes her a little longer to do them. Through their friendship, Charlie and Isabelle are doing their small part to make the world a more tolerant place.

About the author: In 1997 Eliza Woloson established the Global Education Fund, a nonprofit organization that builds libraries in orphanages around the world. She lives in Boulder, Colorado with her husband, Todd, and two children, Isabelle and her younger sister, Audrey.

About the illustrator: Bryan Gough is a designer and artist living and working in Boulder, Colorado. When he is not doing his art, he is raising his son, John.